Forests

Yvonne Franklin

Forests

Publishing Credits

Editorial Director
Dona Herweck Rice

Creative Director
Lee Aucoin

Associate Editor
James Anderson

Illustration Manager
Timothy J. Bradley

Editor-in-Chief
Sharon Coan, M.S.Ed.

Publisher
Rachelle Cracchiolo, M.S.Ed.

Science Consultants
Scot Oschman, Ph.D.
David W. Schroeder, M.S.

Teacher Created Materials

5301 Oceanus Drive
Huntington Beach, CA 92649-1030
http://www.tcmpub.com

ISBN 978-1-4333-0317-3

Table of Contents

Into the Woods 4

What Is a Forest? 8

Life in a Forest.. 14

Forest Cycles.. 20

Renewal 26

Appendices 28

　　　Lab: Ant Farm.. 28

　　　Glossary... 30

　　　Index... 31

　　　Scientists Then and Now.................................. 32

　　　Image Credits... 32

Into the Woods

You walk down a country road. The sun shines warmly on your shoulders. You keep your eyes on the ground ahead. You hear the sound of birds singing.

You step, and something crunches under your feet. It is dried leaves. The ground is grassy and covered with small plants.

You keep walking. You notice it is a little darker now. The air is cooler. Leaves underfoot are wet and rotting away. You look up. Trees are all around you. A squirrel scurries up a tree trunk. Birds sing in the branches above your head. And there, just in front of you, a small black spider spins a large web. The web stretches between two trees. You look at it closely and see the spider's careful work.

You realize now that you have entered a **forest**. It is cool. It is filled with trees, plants, and wildlife. Everything is green, brown, and blue, with splashes of other colors mixed in. The sounds of wind, water, animals, and rustling leaves fill the air.

Woods or Forest?

Are forests and woods the same thing? A woods is a small forest.

4

Types of Forests

There are three main types of forest. They are tropical (near the equator), boreal (far north), and **temperate**. The type of forest described in this book is temperate.

Temperate forests are known for their warm, moist summers and cold, frosty winters.

How do you know that a place is a forest? After all, you can find plants and animals just about anywhere. What makes a forest a forest?

Each place in the world is part of a **biome**. A biome is a large area of land or water. No matter where you find one type of biome, it will have the same kinds of animals, plants, climate, and landscape. A desert is a biome. An ocean is a biome. A forest is a biome, too.

That does not mean that every forest is the same as another forest. There are different types of forests. But they have a lot in common with each other. And a person would never mistake a desert or an ocean for a forest! That may seem obvious, but you may not be able to give the reasons why they are not the same. For example, you might think that deserts are different from forests because they have sand. Forests may have sand, and not every desert has sand. You might think that oceans are different because they have great amounts of water. Well, forests can have a lot of water, too. Not as much as an ocean, but still a lot!

So, how do you know a place is a forest? Read on.

Where Are They?

Temperate forests are found around the world, but they are mostly in North America, Asia, and Europe.

tropic of Cancer

equator

tropic of Capricorn

Legend

temperate forests

equator

Forests, Forests Everywhere

Forest biomes cover about one-third of all the land on Earth.

What Is a Forest?

In a temperate forest biome, the main thing you will see is plenty of trees and other plant life. The plants grow in layers. The upper layer is called the canopy. The canopy covers the other layers. As long as the canopy is not too thick, sunlight can reach the lower layers and allow them to grow.

Low-lying plants cover parts of the forest floor. This is called the litter layer. It is made of plants such as moss and **lichens** (LIE-kuhns). Just above the litter is the fern layer. Ferns and herbs grow there. The shrub layer is just above that. A shrub is smaller than a tree. It usually has several stems that branch from or near the ground. The shrub layer reaches just a few meters from the ground.

Between the shrubs and the canopy is the understory. The understory is made of younger, smaller trees than are found in the canopy.

Forest Differences

A rainforest is a common type of forest, but it is not the same as a temperate forest. For example, in a rainforest the canopy is very thick. In a temperate forest, the canopy is full but not thick.

temperate forest

canopy

understory

shrub layer

fern layer

litter layer

If there are plenty of trees and other plants, does that mean the place is a forest? No. There are some other important things, too.

You will know it is a temperate forest if . . .

- there are many trees and plants over a large area.
- the four seasons are easy to tell apart.
- the climate is not extreme.
- there is a growing season of about 140-200 days each year.
- precipitation falls year round.
- the soil is rich and **fertile** (plants grow easily).
- many different kinds of plants and animals are found there.

Winters can drop to about -30°C (-22°F).

Fading Fast

Temperate forests once covered huge areas of Earth. Only small pieces of those forests remain today. Many have been cleared for housing, businesses, farming, and **logging**.

Summers reach highs of about 30°C (86°F).

Forest Seasons

spring

autumn

Not all temperate forests are the same. There are two main types. They are **deciduous** (di-SID-joo-uhs) and **coniferous** (kuh-NIF-er-uhs).

A deciduous forest is known for its autumn colors. The leaves on trees change color in the fall. They turn from green to shades of yellow, red, orange, and brown. The leaves die and fall from the trees in winter. In spring, new leaves and buds grow. The leaves are full and green in the summer.

A coniferous forest is known for its evergreen trees. The leaves of most evergreen trees do not change color or fall away in winter. The leaves are often needles. The trees stay green. Their seeds are mainly found in cones.

Water

Like other biomes, water can be found in forests. Every forest gets rain, although some get more than others. Many forests have rivers, streams, and ponds in them. Some forests run up to the edges of large lakes.

Seeds can be found within a pinecone such as this one.

coniferous needles

deciduous leaves

Turn a New Leaf

The leaves in the forest equal about two-thirds of all the leaves on Earth! That means that two out of every three leaves are found in forests.

Life in a Forest

A forest is filled with many kinds of plants and animals. They live together in **ecosystems** (EK-oh-sis-tuhms). An ecosystem is a community of living things together with the land, air, and water that they need.

Animals and plants in an ecosystem are connected in energy pyramids. Energy pyramids show how energy is exchanged. One food source exchanges it with another. Plants are at the bottom of most energy pyramids. Most animals eat plants. Some animals eat plants and meat. Some eat only meat.

Animals are **consumers**. They consume, or eat, plants and other animals. A rabbit, a mouse, and a beetle eat some plants. They take the nutrients and energy from the plants and use them to live. Later, a cougar may eat the rabbit. An owl may eat the mouse and beetle. The cougar and owl use the energy and nutrients from the bodies of the other animals. Later, a wolf or wolf pack may eat the cougar and the owl. The transfer of energy continues.

deer

Fauna

Fauna (animal life) in a temperate forest includes deer, wolves, rabbits, foxes, bears, cougars, squirrels, spiders, insects, birds, and more.

honeysuckle

Flora

Flora (plant life) in a temperate forest includes trees such as elm, willow, oak, beech, birch, maple, pine, spruce, firs, and hemlock; shrubs such as honeysuckle, juniper, dogwood, chokeberry, sumac, and sage; and other plant life such as ferns, herbs, moss, and lichens.

Energy Pyramid

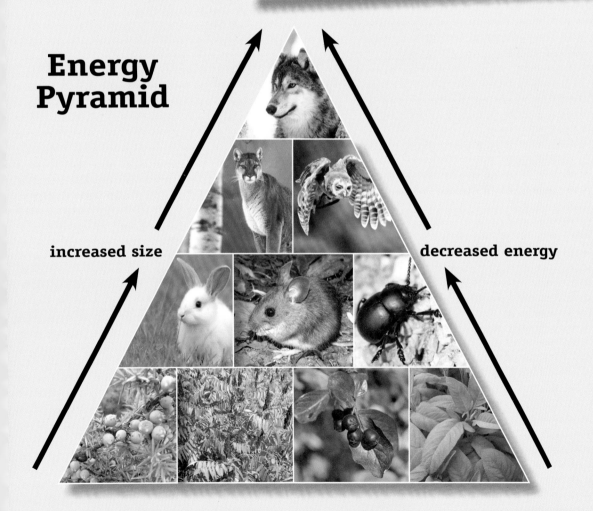

increased size

decreased energy

At some point, the wolf will die. Its body will rot away. **Decomposers** such as worms, bacteria, and **fungi** (FUHNG-gahy) will break down the wolf's dead body. They will use the energy from the body. They will return the nutrients to the earth. Plants will use the nutrients to grow.

Energy is shared at every step of the pyramid. But most of the energy is lost as it is passed from one level to the next. Animals use about one-fifth of the energy that is in their food. Take a look at the energy pyramid on the last page. The animals at the top of the energy pyramid get their energy from other animals. They get the energy that has become weaker as it is passed from plant to animal to animal. Since animals at the top of the pyramid receive less energy, they need to eat more to survive. An ecosystem may only be able to support a few large animals at the top of the energy pyramid. Animals at the lower levels of the energy pyramid get their energy from the source (plants). There is more energy at the bottom of the energy pyramid. Smaller animals can survive in greater numbers because of this.

Yum! Shrubs!

In a forest, much of the food for animals is found in the shrub layer of plants. And because most things in nature are parts of connected **cycles**, many shrubs depend on the animals that eat them to distribute their seeds. How do the animals do it? They eat the fruit of the plants, and then the seeds are placed throughout the forest in the animals' feces (FEE-seez). It's nature's very own fertilizer!

These decomposers are breaking down the organism's body and using the energy to live.

You will find many more small animals, such as these ants, in an ecosystem than large animals.

But an energy pyramid does not tell the whole food story. It shows just a few plants and animals. Many more plants and animals are involved in the exchange of energy in an ecosystem. To see more, take a look at a food web.

As the food web shows, many plants and animals are strongly connected to each other. There is an exchange of energy among them. The arrows show the flow of energy.

The truth is, this food web shows only a small part of the energy exchange in a forest. A complete food web would include much more than this. Think of other forest animals and plants that you know. Where would they fit in this web? How would they exchange energy with the other plants and animals?

sun

Forest Fast Food

Sunlight in a forest must pass through the top layers to reach the bottom layers. So, there is less sunlight available on the forest floor. That is one reason why low lying plants tend to have shorter life spans. Also, they are within easy reach of many animals. Think of them as nature's fast food restaurants!

Forest Food Web

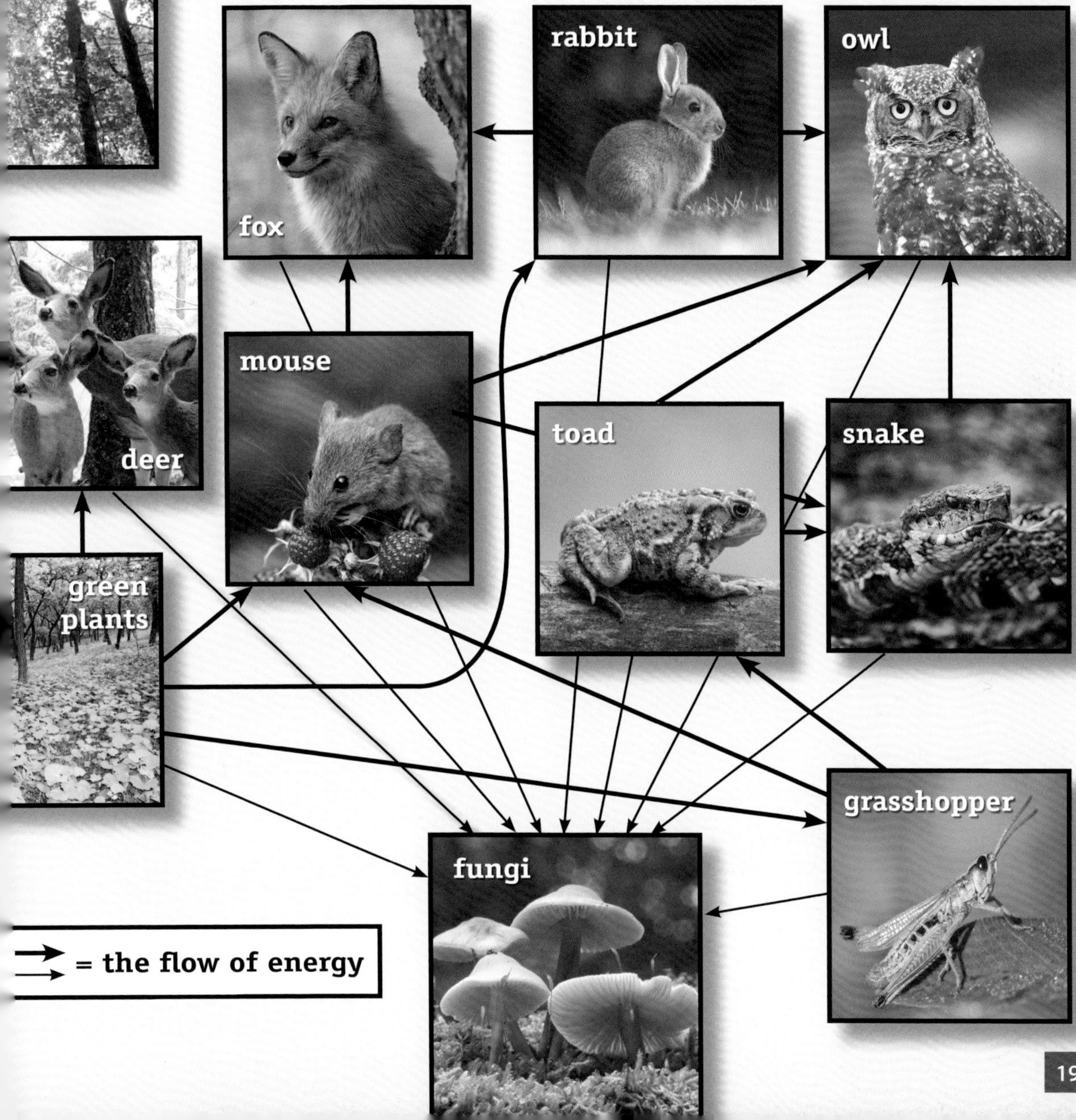

fox

rabbit

owl

mouse

deer

toad

snake

green plants

fungi

grasshopper

= the flow of energy

This deer and fawn, and seedling and tree, are part of life cycles found in a forest.

Cycles in Nature

Anywhere on Earth, you will find a variety of natural cycles. The water cycle, the seasons, and the cycle of day and night are among the most common and easy to recognize cycles. Throughout the day, look around you. What signs do you see of each of these cycles?

Forest Cycles

Energy pyramids and food webs show how things connect to each other in an ecosystem. Plants and animals need one another to survive. Some people call this the circle of life.

There are many other such circles, or **cycles**, in a forest. A cycle is something that follows from start to finish and back again. It repeats over and over. The life of an animal is part of a cycle. It goes from beginning to end. During its lifetime, the animal has babies. In this way, the cycle continues. It is the same way for a plant. A plant's life goes from beginning to end, but the plant creates new seedlings. The cycle continues.

You may know a great deal about the life cycle of many animals. Frogs begin as eggs and then become tadpoles. Caterpillars become butterflies. Some animals such as deer grow antlers as adults.

The life cycle of a plant is interesting, too. Trees are especially so. You can see the cycle of a tree's life just by looking at it closely!

A tree grows in layers. Each layer from the outer bark to the core has a job to do.

The outer bark protects the tree. It keeps the tree from getting too much moisture. It also protects the tree from insects. Food travels through the tree in the inner bark. The **cambium** layer is the part that lets a tree grow. It grows new bark on the outside of itself and new wood on the inside. The new bark and wood make the tree grow thicker each year.

Water moves through the tree to the leaves in the sapwood layer. The sapwood is also the newest wood of the tree. The core of the tree is called the heartwood. It is the strong center that helps to hold the huge weight of the tree.

Ah, Life!

The only living cells in the trunk of a tree are found in the cambium layer.

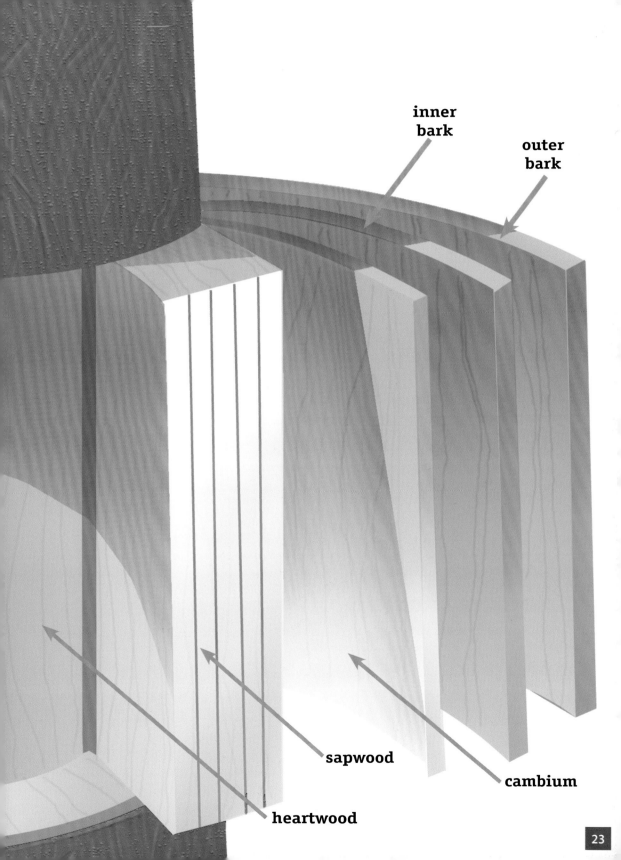

inner
bark

outer
bark

sapwood

cambium

heartwood

The layers of the tree can be seen in a cross section, like the one shown here. The layers are called rings.

If you look closely at the rings, you can see the life story of the tree. The center shows the first growth of the tree. Wide rings show years of healthy growth with plenty of rain and nutrients. Narrow rings show years of less water and sunlight. They can also show disease or insect trouble. Scarring that has new wood growth over it may mean that there was a forest fire with some damage to the tree. But the new growth means the tree became healthy again.

There is a reason for the light and dark shades in a tree's rings. New wood grows in the spring and summer. Wood in the spring grows fast. The cells are large and light. Summer growth is slower. The cells are **dense** and dark.

As a tree grows, it produces flowers and then seeds. The seeds fall to the ground. Some of the seeds sprout and become new trees. The new trees have new rings and new stories to tell. The circle of life continues.

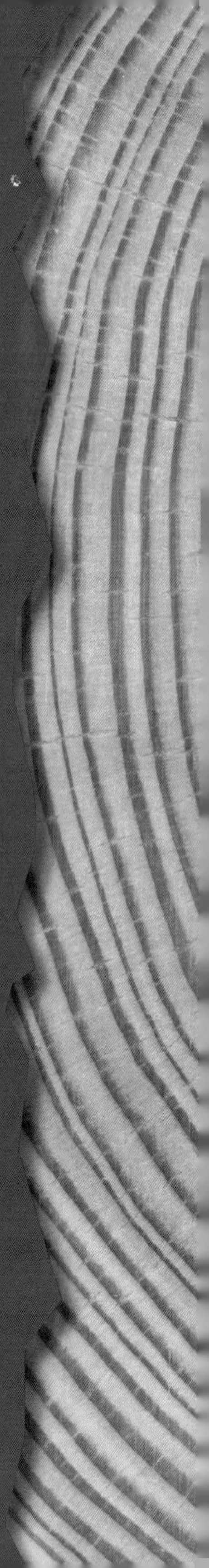

Happy Birthday!

You can figure out a tree's age by counting its dark rings.

rings

Trees may have narrow rings because they are crowded. Some trees take more of the available water and energy from the sun. This causes other trees to grow less.

People

People can either harm or help a forest. Pollution and too much logging can permanently damage a forest. But people can also work to replant, protect, and restore forests.

The bleakness after a forest fire does not last for long. New life springs up as soon as it can. A forest will always try to bring itself back to health.

Renewal

One of the most amazing cycles in a forest is the way that it renews itself. Fires, floods, **droughts** (drowts), and storms are a natural part of forest life. Each of these things can change a forest.

Fires might clear the land of plant life. Floods can erode, or wear away, the land. Droughts slow growth, while some plants die and some animals move away. Storms may topple trees. But a forest has ways of dealing with all these things. Shortly after a fire, new growth begins to pop up through the soil. As flood waters recede, plant and animal life adapts to the changed landscape. Most droughts end at some point, and water returns to the land. Decomposers break down toppled trees. Nutrients are released to the soil for other plants to use.

It is almost as though the job of a forest is to live and grow. The cycle of life just goes on and on.

Lab: Ant Farm

One of the best ways to learn about cycles in nature is to observe them. Some of nature's smallest creatures have some of the most fascinating lives! Ants, for example, are well organized and work hard all their lives. You can build an ant farm to observe how ants live. Be sure to treat the ants with respect. They are living things, after all.

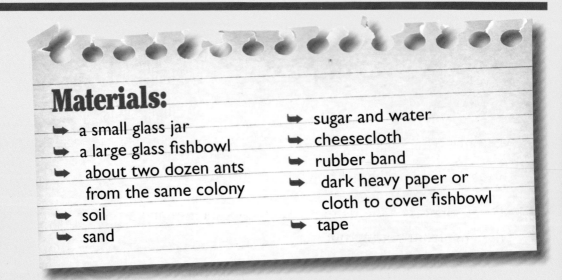

Materials:

- a small glass jar
- a large glass fishbowl
- about two dozen ants from the same colony
- soil
- sand
- sugar and water
- cheesecloth
- rubber band
- dark heavy paper or cloth to cover fishbowl
- tape

Procedure:

1. Carefully collect about two dozen ants from a single colony. If they are not from the same colony, they will fight.

2. Put the small glass jar upside down inside the large fishbowl.

3. Mix soil and sand so that it is loose. Pour it into the fishbowl.

4. Mix a little water and sugar together. Use the eyedropper to put several drops of the mixture in the sandy soil.

5. Add the ants to the fishbowl.

6. Cover the lid of the fishbowl with cheesecloth and a rubber band to keep the ants from getting out.

7. Wrap the dark paper or cloth around the fishbowl and tape it in place. This will make the ants think they are in the dark underground.

8. Store the fishbowl at room temperature someplace quiet. Each day, add some drops of water to the soil. Each week, add some drops of sugar water. (Just drop the water or sugar water on the surface this time.)

9. Take off the dark covering each day to observe what the ants are doing. They will begin to build tunnels and make rooms in just a few days. Be sure to cover them up again soon so that you do not disturb them.

10. Write what you see. What do you notice about ants?

Glossary

biome—a large area of land or water that has common types of plants, animals, climate and landscape

cambium—the living layer of a tree that grows new bark and new wood

coniferous—a type of temperate forest in which cone-bearing and evergreen trees grow

consumers—organisms that eat or take nutrients from other organisms

cycle—a periodically repeated sequence of events

deciduous—a type of temperate forest in which leaves are shed each year

decomposers—organisms that break down other organisms

dense—tightly compacted

droughts—times of low or no new water coming to a wide area of land

ecosystem—a geographical area where plants, animals, land, and weather all interact together

fauna—animal life

fertile—able to grow new life

flora—plant life

forest—a large area of land covered with trees and brush

fungi—simple organisms that decay and absorb the matter from the organisms on which they live

lichens—fungi that grow on rocks and tree trunks

logging—the process or business of cutting down trees and bringing them to mills for manufacturing

temperate—a type of forest marked by generally cool and mild temperatures

Index

ants, 28–29

bark, 22–23

biome, 6–8, 12

cambium, 22–23

canopy, 8–9

coniferous, 12–13

consumers, 14

cycles, 16, 20, 21, 27

deciduous, 12–13

decomposers, 16–17, 27

ecosystem, 14, 16–18, 21

energy pyramid, 14–16, 18, 21

fauna, 14

fern layer, 8–9

flora, 15

food webs, 18–19, 21

leaves, 4, 11–13, 22

litter layer, 8–9

logging, 10, 26

rainforest, 8

rings, 24–25

seasons, 10–11, 20

shrub layer, 8–9, 16

temperate, 5–6, 8, 10–12, 14–15

trees, 4, 8, 10, 12, 15, 21, 24–25, 27

understory, 8–9

Scientists Then and Now

John Muir
(1838–1914)

Jessica L. Deichmann
(1980–)

John Muir was born in Scotland. He always loved nature. As a young man, John began attending "the university of the wilderness." He learned by seeing things for himself. He traveled to Yosemite Valley in California to explore nature there. He wanted to protect the valley for the future. So, he helped make it a national park. He also helped form the Sierra Club. It is a group devoted to protecting nature.

Jessica Deichmann is an ecologist. She studies nature and the environment. She especially loves to learn about frogs, lizards, and snakes. She travels a lot to see these creatures in their own environments. She also teaches people how to help protect the animals. Jessica does everything she can to protect wildlife now and for the future.

Image Credits